The Witch of Bloor Street

by

Beth Pollock

James Lorimer & Company Ltd., Publishers
Toronto

Copyright © 2010 by Beth Pollock
First published in the United States in 2011.

All rights reserved. No part of this book may be reproduced or transmitted in
any form or by any means, electronic or mechanical, including photocopying,
or by any information storage or retrieval system, without permission in writing from the publisher.

James Lorimer & Company Ltd., Publishers acknowledges the support of the
Ontario Arts Council. We acknowledge the financial support of the Government
of Canada through the Canada Book Fund for our publishing activities. We
acknowledge the support of the Canada Council for the Arts for our publishing program. We acknowledge the Government of Ontario through the Ontario
Media Development Corporation's Ontario Book Initiative.

The Canada Council | Le Conseil des Arts
for the Arts | du Canada

ONTARIO ARTS COUNCIL
CONSEIL DES ARTS DE L'ONTARIO

Cover design: Meredith Bangay   Front cover image: iStock

Library and Archives Canada Cataloguing in Publication

Pollock, Beth
The witch of Bloor Street / by Beth Pollock.

(Streetlights)
Issued also in an electronic format.
ISBN 978-1-55277-536-3

I. Title. II. Series: Streetlights

PS8631.O45W58 2010   jC813'.6   C2010-902614-4

James Lorimer & Company Ltd.,   Distributed in the
Publishers   United States by:
317 Adelaide Street West,   Orca Book Publishers
Suite 1002   P.O. Box 468
Toronto, ON, Canada, M5V 1P9   Custer, WA U.S.A.
www.lorimer.ca   98240-0468

Printed and bound in Canada.
Manufactured by Webcom in Toronto, Ontario, Canada in August 2010.
Job # 370663

In honour of my sister, Gwen McDermott.

1

Hi Maggie,

My name is Mrs. Fedorchuk, and I'm going to be your sixth-grade teacher this year. I'll be exchanging e-mail throughout the year with all of my students, and I look forward to getting to know you better. Can you tell me a little about yourself? Do you have any brothers or sisters? What is one goal you have for grade six? What are you planning to do for your last week of the summer holidays?

I'll tell you a few things about myself. My favourite summer memory was visiting my sister in Prince Edward Island. I love animals, and I have two terriers named Eddie and Freddie. And I'm spending the last week of summer getting my classroom ready!

Enjoy the rest of the summer.
Mrs. Fedorchuk

Dear Mrs. Fedorchuk,

Hi! I'm Maggie, and I'm eleven years old. I have an older sister, Mary. She's fifteen and she's really bossy.

My goal for sixth grade is to become the best at something. I'm good at lots of things, but not best at anything.

In the last week before school, I hope to visit a dragon sanctuary. If I'm brave, I'll go into a haunted house.

See you next week!
Maggie Ito

I can't wait to have Mrs. Fedorchuk as a teacher. She sent me this e-mail today to introduce herself. I already know who she is, though. Mrs. Fedorchuk used to teach grade one, and the little kids always wanted to hold her hand. She even has dimples when she smiles. She'd be a perfect fairy godmother.

There are only five days left until the first day of school. On Monday, my family and I got back from vacation, but my best friend, Sasha Kovalik, is still at camp so I don't have much to do. Every time I tell

Dad I'm bored, he says, "Help me fold the laundry" or "Why don't you unload the dishwasher?"

But at lunch he gives me a different answer. "How about walking up to Runnymede library and getting some books?" he says. "You'll be walking home from school by yourself this year. You can practise this afternoon."

I've been looking forward to walking to school by myself since Mary was in grade six. As soon as the table is cleared from lunch, I quickly lace up my runners, worried that Dad will change his mind.

"Come back with something to read, or I'll have to find more laundry for you to fold," he says with a wink.

Most days I'll walk to school with Sasha, but today I feel like a true adventurer. As I race out the door and tear down our street, I'm glad to be wearing a sweater. It's been a cold, wet summer, and today is no different. I hope I get back before it rains.

Despite the weather, it's a great afternoon for two reasons: I'm going to Bloor Street by myself, and I'm going to check out Fresh Ink — or, as I call it, the haunted house. I've been waiting for the day I could walk up and investigate it on my own.

That day is today.

Whenever my family goes to High Park, we walk past Fresh Ink. The sign says it's a tattoo parlour, but I'm sure it's really a haunted house. I never see people walking in or out, and one of the windows is covered with a picture of a skull. Maybe they have a door knocker that comes to life when you use it. I wonder if there are ghosts floating around, or cobwebs on the furniture.

But first, the library. No matter what perils await me at Fresh Ink, I need something to do when I get home.

I head to the kids' section and choose *Fablehaven* and *The Hobbit*. Wouldn't it be great to live in a magical world like the ones in those books? Sometimes I think I really do, but I just can't see it yet.

Maybe that magical world is in the playground beside the library. I peer out the picture window and imagine it's actually a dragon sanctuary that's been enchanted by a powerful wizard. If the spell is lifted, I'll see two enormous dragons clashing over a hoard of gold and jewels, buried deep below the sandbox. I squint, hoping to glimpse a little of the sanctuary, but all I see is a slide and a couple of swings. I can't find danger anywhere in my neighbourhood.

I walk half a block to the haunted house. It's separated from the library by a couple of vacant buildings, and it sits back from the street, unlike the other shops which come right up to the sidewalk. The skull in the window leers at me, daring me to approach the door. The sign in front reads:

Fresh Ink
Tattoos and Piercings
— With or Without Appointments —

I wonder if the people who go in for an appointment ever come out again.

The path leading to the doorway is overgrown. Flowers spill out of the sides of their planters and droop toward the ground, struggling to escape their cement prisons. The front lawn is a mess of dark green grass, growing thick and matted. I can hardly breathe for the smell of over-ripe flowers.

A gust of wind wafts up the walk and a few dark clouds have floated in from the distance. I pull the sweater tighter around myself, clutching my library books. I'd better make this quick.

I pick my way along the path, until I reach the front door. There's no knocker, but there is a handle. I gulp, tug the door open, and glance inside. Tattoo designs cover the walls: flying eagles, huge-headed snakes, spindly spiders. I feel like I've landed in the middle of a giant graphic novel, without the captions.

I hear someone coming up the sidewalk behind me. I step through the doorway and into the middle of the room to let him pass. Both his arms are covered in swirling designs and initials. He has a goatee and is wearing a black baseball cap. He catches me watching him so I look away, pretending to choose a design. If he's here for another tattoo, where will he put it? Maybe he has room on his elbows.

There's a curtain hung across a doorway at the back of the room, and a door at the right that's open about an inch. A blazing light shines through the gap, and I walk toward it. What's making that light? A magical orb? A gateway to another world? But when I peek through the opening, I realize it's just a bright overhead light reflecting off white walls. There's a reclining leather chair and, against the wall, there's a counter with a bunch of bottles lined up. It's as tidy as a hair salon — and just as safe.

This isn't what I expected. Where are the ghosts, the cobwebs? The floor doesn't even creak! It isn't dangerous at all.

Suddenly, I hear a cackle of laughter coming from behind the curtain, and the sound of footsteps approaching. I gasp and lurch backwards. What am I doing here? What if it really *is* dangerous?

I'm ready to escape when the curtain is swept back and two shapes emerge from the shadowy room beyond. One is a skinny guy with barbed wire tattooed around his arm. He says hi to the guy with the goatee, like they are old friends. But they aren't the ones I'm staring at.

A woman with cherry-red hair and lipstick to match stands next to them. She wears a thick bronze ring through her lower lip. Above her neckline, I can see the brilliant pink and green of her tattoo. She's dressed in black, from her T-shirt right down to her work boots. She cackles again, and my teeth chatter.

She must be a witch!

If I've learned anything from books, it's not to

panic when faced with a problem. I can only hope that the witch and her henchman will overlook me long enough to let me escape. On shaking legs, I drift to the front counter, away from everyone else, pretending to look at the jewelry. When I'm closer to the door, I'll make a run for it and stay away forever.

The two men chat as they walk into the tattooing room with the reclining chair. I can't bear to turn around — the red-haired witch and I are alone. How will I get away?

"Can I help you?"

I'm startled by her voice. It rasps like an unoiled hinge. I can barely breathe. I definitely can't speak.

"Are you here for a tattoo?"

I turn around to see her staring at me. I wonder what she's thinking. Did she ask Hansel and Gretel the same question when she lured them into the gingerbread house?

I try to say no, I don't want a tattoo, but nothing comes out. All I can do is shake my head as I back away from her. And suddenly I crash into the counter.

Visa sign, skeleton pins, earrings and nose rings scatter all over the floor.

Time to disappear. I tuck the books under my arm and bolt out of the shop.

"Hey, wait, come back . . ." The witch's voice fades as I tear away from the shop.

Just as I'm sprinting toward safety, I catch my toe in a crack in the sidewalk and go sprawling, books flying in every direction. *Fablehaven* sails into the street, and I watch as a sports car drives over it. I leap to my feet and grab the book before anyone else hits it. It's still in one piece, but it has a damp brown tire tread on the back cover. Limping back to the sidewalk, I rub my sore knees and examine my skinned palms.

It's only when I bring my sore hand closer to my face that I spot something dangling from my sleeve. A tiny silver broomstick earring is clinging to my sweater.

I unhook the earring and hold it in my palm. It must have gotten snagged when I knocked the display over. I know I should take it back. But that would mean seeing the witch again. *Nothing* could convince me to do that.

I put the earring in my pocket while I think about

what to do next.

Bit by bit, the rain that's been threatening all day starts to fall and soon it's a downpour. I protect the books as well as I can and race home. But by the time I get there, I'm a mess. My hair is dripping wet. My hands and knees are aching from my fall. And my library book has been run over by a car.

There's only one explanation for the state I'm in. I've been cursed by a real-life witch.

2

Dear Maggie,

    I have an older sister, too. When I was in grade six she was bossy, but she helped me a lot with homework.

    Your final week of summer sounds wonderful. Did you visit the dragon sanctuary and the haunted house?

Mrs. Fedorchuk

Dear Mrs. Fedorchuk,

    I couldn't get into the dragon sanctuary, but I went into the haunted house. Unfortunately, while I was there a witch cast an evil spell on me.

    Can you tell me how to get rid of a curse?

Maggie Ito

P.S. Mary is bossy, but she is not helpful.

I always love the first day of school. My pencil crayons are still sharp. My binder rings still close properly. Jarrett Johnson hasn't stolen my eraser yet and written *girls suck* on it.

I knew I could tell Mrs. Fedorchuk about the witch. Some adults don't understand that kind of thing. Last year, my teacher told me that people my age don't believe in fairy tales so I should write stories about my family. But I was positive Mrs. Fedorchuk would like hearing about the witch, and I was right.

Maybe this is going to be a good year, curse or no curse.

It would be a great year if I figured out what I'm best at. My friends are all best at something. Sasha is the most talented artist. Lauren is fastest at math. Alice is the best singer. Even Jarrett Johnson — who is *not* my friend — is the fastest runner in sixth grade. And the biggest pest.

"Thanks to all of you who responded to my e-mail last week," Mrs. Fedorchuk says. "This term I'll be exchanging letters by e-mail with each of you. It's a good way for you to practise your writing skills, and for me to get to know you."

A wave of groans washes over the room. But I don't mind. It's better than exchanging extra math assignments by e-mail.

Sasha leans over and whispers, "Are you okay?" She isn't talking about the e-mail assignment, or the tensor bandage on my right arm, which I've been wearing since I tripped outside the haunted house. What she means is, "Have you recovered from attendance yet?" Every year on the first day of school, the new teacher reads the attendance list, and when she gets to the M's, she says, "Is Magnolia Ito here?" That reminds everyone that my real name is totally embarrassing, and some of them will call me Magnolia for the next week or two. I've asked Mrs. Fedorchuk to call me Maggie, but this morning she did what all teachers do the first day of school. Now I'm just waiting for somebody else to tease me about my name.

Out of the corner of my eye, I see something disappearing from my table. Jarrett's outstretched hand is scooping up my eraser.

"Give that back!" I whisper.

He smirks.

"I mean it!" I hiss.

Sasha kicks me under the table, and I pivot to see Mrs. Fedorchuk smiling at me.

"Are you still with us, Maggie?" she asks. I nod and sit up straight. When she turns around, I glance at Jarrett, who is laughing at me without making a sound.

If Mrs. Fedorchuk really was my fairy godmother, she'd wave a wand and change Jarrett into a toad. If the witch of Bloor Street was here, she'd give him a poisoned apple. But it doesn't look like either is going to happen. As usual, I have to deal with Jarrett by myself.

Maybe the first day of school isn't so great after all.

Every year since grade two Jarrett has stolen my eraser during the first couple of weeks of school. But this year, he's managed to steal it on day one.

Having my eraser stolen doesn't sound serious, especially when it happens every year. But there's more. On the weekend, I accidentally let our cat Neko sneak out of the house, and I had to chase her down the street. Last night, Dad made meatloaf for dinner — and served it with sweet potatoes. Bad luck doesn't get much worse than that. And this morning,

I was at the end of my street when I realized I'd for-gotten to bring my lunch. I had to run back and grab it from the counter, which almost made Sasha and me late on the first day of school. If that happens, you might as well kiss the good luck fairy good-bye.

I bring my mind back to the classroom. Mrs. Fedorchuk is finishing a discussion about individual responsibility. I doubt I missed much. We hear one of those lectures every year.

Every time Mrs. Fedorchuk looks away, Jarrett tosses my eraser in the air. I grit my teeth. "Why can't he leave my stuff alone?" I whisper to Sasha. "He's like a troll, stealing other people's stuff for no reason."

"Crabby, ugly, takes things — you might be onto something."

When the bell rings at 3:30, Sasha and I pick up our binders. I haven't told anyone but her about the earring, and she's coming to my place after school to see it.

As Mrs. Fedorchuk turns to pack her briefcase, Jarrett whips the eraser at us. Sasha ducks and I make a mid-air catch.

"Nice catch, *Magnolia*," Jarrett says, walking out of the room.

I flip the eraser over. *Girls suck* is engraved on the back in huge block letters.

"I hate him," I say.

First day of school, and already Jarrett has stolen, defaced, and returned my eraser. He has also mocked me behind the teacher's back, called me 'Magnolia,' and made sure I got caught asking for my eraser back.

If that isn't proof of a curse, I don't know what is.

3

Dear Maggie,

You are so creative! I would love to see you write stories about the witch who cursed you. Later this fall I'll be assigning creative writing projects, and this would be a perfect subject. In the meantime, I hope your sore wrist doesn't make it difficult to type these e-mails.

I meant to ask you about your goal to be best at something. Is there anything in particular that you want to be best at?
Mrs. Fedorchuk

Dear Mrs. Fedorchuk,

My wrist doesn't bother me that much. I can do most of the things I normally do, just more slowly. Fortunately, that means I can type. Unfortunately, it also means I can unload the dishwasher.

Some of the things I like to do are reading, taking pictures, and playing with my cat, Neko. Some of the things I'd like to be best at are defeating trolls, entering dragon sanctuaries, and standing up to witches.
Maggie

Dad's usually at home before and after school. He designs websites, so he works while Mary and I are away. Mom puts in long hours at the bank and gets home after dinner most nights. Most of my friends say their dads are awful cooks, but my dad is the best cook around. Except when he makes meatloaf and sweet potatoes.

I pick at the edge of my tensor bandage. "I'm sick of wearing this," I say. "Can I take it off?"

Dad shakes his head. "Dr. Cameron said you should wear it a full week. You can leave it off tomorrow morning."

Wearing this bandage has been a pain. It makes everything a hundred times harder to do. I can't play any hand games with Sasha. We tried doing Slide with one hand, but it wasn't the same. At least it's my right arm — being left-handed, I can still write.

Also, it's impossible to braid my hair with one hand. Dad offered to help, but he'd be worse with two hands than I am with one. Luckily, Mom told Mary she has to do my braids until my bandage is off. Mary does such a good job, I'm tempted to wear the bandage longer than I have to.

I pick up Sasha on the way to school. As we meet in front of her house I see two other grade sixers ahead of us. Annica and Nathaniel are walking to school hand-in-hand, about half a block ahead. I whisper, "What are they *doing*?"

"Didn't you hear?" Sasha asks. "They're dating. Some of the kids gave them a mashup name — Nathannica."

"Dating?" I make a face. "Why would they do that?"

"I don't know. Mom says someday I'll like boys, but I don't believe it."

"Mary told me the boys in grade ten are just like the boys in grade six. All they care about are video games, sports, and food. I am *never* going to have a boyfriend."

As we walk into the schoolyard, we see Jarrett and

Lionel trying to push each other into a puddle.

"See what I mean?" I say to Sasha. "And the boys in grade six are like the boys in grade two."

"Let's get out of here before they splash us. I have a math question for Mrs. Fedorchuk. Want to come in with me?"

We head in, and Sasha goes into the classroom to speak to the teacher. I'm hanging around the lockers waiting for her to come out when I see that Jarrett has left the padlock on his locker hanging open.

I check both ways. No one's in sight. It's payback time.

I grab his lock and stick it on my top shelf. Then I put *my* lock on his locker and close it. He'll never be able to get in.

As I finish up, Mrs. Fedorchuk comes out of the classroom followed by Sasha. Did anyone see what I was doing? I blush, but Mrs. Fedorchuk doesn't say a thing. I'm safe.

The bell rings, and the rest of the students pile into the school as I saunter into homeroom. A minute or two later, I hear Jarrett complaining out in the hall, "I can't open my locker."

Mrs. Fedorchuk's calm voice says, "Try again, Jarrett. You're probably going too quickly."

"I've tried four times already. Something's wrong with this lock!"

Pause. Then Mrs. Fedorchuk's face appears at the door. "Maggie, can you join us in the hall for a minute, please?"

Busted! I can't believe it. I slink out to meet her.

"Maggie, do you have something that belongs to Jarrett?"

I don't say a word. I shuffle to my locker and return his padlock.

"You'll have to open Jarrett's locker for him, too."

I ignore his gloating face as I spin the combination. He really is a troll. I bet he lives under a bridge and eats billy goats.

"Guys," Mrs. Fedorchuk says, "there's been a lot of teasing going on in both directions. I want you to leave each other alone."

We both nod.

When I return to class, Sasha makes a face. "Poor you. It's the curse, isn't it?"

"Yup."

"Maggie, you've gotta get rid of it. Do you have any ideas?"

"Nope."

"Why don't you ask your parents what to do?"

It's a good suggestion, but I can't do that — I'm not sure why I can't. Partly it's because I don't want to mention the haunted house. It would be hard to explain who I was running from, and why she brought me bad luck. But the main reason is that my family treats me like a baby. Mary acts as if her problems are more important than mine. She'll be stressed out over a French exam, but if I tell her I'm studying for French, too, she'll roll her eyes and say "Puh-lease."

If I tell my family that I went in a tattoo parlour and a witch chased me out, Mary would say, "You're too old to believe in witches," and Mom and Dad would say, "You're too young to go in a tattoo parlour."

And nobody would take me seriously.

"I have to figure this out without telling them," I say. Kids stream into the class around us, kids with uncursed lives. Kids with good luck instead of bad. Wait a minute . . . *good luck*!

"That's it!" I say. "I can't believe I didn't think of

this before. All I need is a good luck charm."

"You mean a lucky penny?"

"Or a four-leaf clover or anything else that brings good luck."

The morning announcements bellow over the intercom. I'm positive this is the perfect solution. Forget one charm. I'll find as many as I can, and bring them into school on Monday. No amount of bad luck can withstand the force of all that good luck!

Dear Maggie,

What a great list of things you'd love to be best at! You definitely set your goals high. Defeating trolls and visiting dragon sanctuaries are hard to do even without a sprained arm.
Mrs. Fedorchuk

Dear Mrs. Fedorchuk,

Good news! On Saturday morning I finally took my tensor bandage off for good! You'll see on Monday. Now I can tie my own shoelaces again. I can braid my hair without listening to Mary complain about it. Best of all, I can play Slide with Sasha.

And I think I know how to get rid of the witch's curse.
Maggie

I spend Saturday and Sunday searching for charms. The lucky penny is easy — it's actually a lucky loonie. Every winter, Dad and I bury a loonie in the backyard rink to bring the Toronto Maple Leafs good luck. We use the same coin every year, and in the off-season we keep it in an ice cube tray in the basement freezer. Once the ice cube around it has melted, I store the loonie in my change purse and set it inside my backpack.

The chances of me finding a four-leaf clover on our lawn are pretty small, but I search anyway. I can only remember one clover that I might use, and I need to go into Mom's cedar chest to get it. Along with some of the other baby clothes she's saved is a Saint Patrick's Day bib with a shamrock on it. It's a three-leaf clover, but the humiliation of carrying a bib to school must be worth at least another leaf. If anyone sees it, I'll never live it down.

At dinner on Saturday night, I have another great idea. Mom serves a roast chicken, and I remember how Mary and I always get the turkey wishbone at Christmas. I don't know where to find the wishbone but, as with the other charms, I'm sure I can improvise.

"Can I have a leg?" I ask.

"Since when do you like dark meat?" Mom says.

"I'll give it a try."

She's right. I don't like dark meat, but I nibble at the leg anyway. After dinner when I'm clearing my plate into the compost bin, I wait until nobody's watching and then I scrub the bone clean and toss it into a baggie. The baggie goes into my backpack, hidden under some books so that if Neko smells it she won't be able to drag it out of my bag. It isn't a wishbone, but it's close enough.

It feels as if I need one more charm. After dinner, I comb through my jewelry box, looking for anything that might bring me luck. I notice the broomstick earring and gently lift it out. That's not the kind of luck I'm looking for. Besides, I could never wear it. It doesn't belong to me, and I don't have the courage to give it back to its owner. I put it back in the jewelry box.

Then I remember Dad's lucky Blue Jays' cap. He wore it both times the Jays won the World Series, and it's signed by Joe Carter. I sneak into his closet and root around at the back until I find it.

It looks like Dad wore it in at least one world war.

It's greasy and beaten up because he sometimes turns it inside out for good luck. He calls it his "rally cap," but Mary and I secretly call it the "smelly cap."

I hold it between my thumb and index finger. The cap has almost totally lost its shape. It's hard to believe that something this grubby is lucky, but if Dad thinks it is, how can I argue? Once I drop it into my backpack with the other things, my job is complete.

Everything seems more complicated at school on Monday. The chicken leg has dried out and now it feels shriveled and rubbery. And I can't exactly hide Dad's hat inside my binder. I stuff the chicken bone in my pencil case, my change purse with the lucky loonie goes in my math workbook, the bib travels in my pocket, and I wear the smelly cap. Good thing I don't have a mirror in my locker, because I don't want to see how bad it looks on me. At least I'm wearing it right-side out.

I slink into the classroom. The cap keeps slipping down over my eyes because Dad's head is bigger than mine. Keeping it off my face will be a challenge.

If I'm *really* lucky, nobody will recognize me. Next to me, Jarrett whispers something to Anthony. I remember to remove my cap when we stand for

"O Canada" but smack it back on my head as soon as we're done singing.

"Class, open your math workbooks to page fifteen," Mrs. Fedorchuk says, standing beside me.

Feeling rattled, I accidentally dump the contents of my pencil case on the ground. My pencil crayons roll up and down the aisle. My eraser bounces up and I catch it before Jarrett can steal it again. The leg bone lands at Mrs. Fedorchuk's feet.

As she leans over to examine it, Jarrett says, "Cool! Where's the rest of the skeleton?"

Mrs. Fedorchuk wrinkles her nose. "Maggie, what is this?"

"My good luck chicken bone," I say.

"It's a bit distracting. Why don't you leave it in your locker until lunchtime?"

"What about the other charms?"

"Others? How many did you bring?"

I reveal the lucky loonie and tug the bib out of my front pocket, making sure no one else sees it. I lean toward her so the others can't hear. "That's why I'm wearing my Dad's baseball cap," I say.

"For good luck?" she asks.

I nod. She smiles and her dimples show. "Keep them in your locker until recess, please. You can wear the hat at recess and lunch for luck. The chicken bone should stay in your locker until the end of the day."

Mrs. Fedorchuk was nice about it, but I wish I could carry my charms with me. Leaving them in my locker might weaken their power.

When the recess bell rings, I'm the first one out in the hall. By the time Sasha joins me, I already have the Blue Jays' cap on. I'm wearing it inside out to make up for lost time.

"Wow," she says. "Are you going to recess wearing that?"

"I can't believe it either, but I need luck any way it comes."

When we get outside, I hunch against the fence at the far end of the schoolyard. It seems as if everyone is staring at me. "Do I really look that bad?" I ask.

"Pretty much."

I'm nearly ready to yank off the cap and admit defeat when I feel it being plucked from my head. I whip around to see Jarrett streaking off with Dad's hat in his hand.

"Hey!" I yell, and run after him. "Give it back!"

Jarrett runs away with the hat, and I swear he's going through the wettest part of the schoolyard on purpose. The legs of my jeans are soaked. And he's such a fast runner, I can't take any detours around puddles or I'll lose him. We run through a grade two game of four-square. "Sorry!" I shout, trying to avoid knocking over a couple of little girls.

He slows down when he gets to the kindergarten wing and I think I have him cornered, but he tosses the cap frisbee-style onto the roof.

"Why did you do that?" I fume.

Jarrett shrugs. He races off and joins the football game at the other side of the yard.

Sasha finally catches up to me. Together we gaze at the bill of the cap, which peeks over the edge of the roof.

"If you lose that hat, your dad's gonna be super-mad." Even Sasha knows about the smelly cap.

"I have to find a caretaker. Do you see Rick?" We search the schoolyard, but it looks like both the caretakers are inside.

"Let's check in the school," Sasha says. "Usually

at least one of them is in their office." She pauses. "I'll come with you, but you do the talking." We rush into the school and head down the hall to knock on the dark green door.

There are two caretakers at our school. Rick is friendly, fun, and jokes with us. But it's Gary who answers the door. Gary has two expressions — scowling and frowning — and most of us are afraid of him. That's why Sasha said she wasn't going to do any talking. But I have to get that hat off the roof, and only Gary can help me.

After I explain what happened, Gary growls, "You kids. Always throwing your things on the roof. Why don't you take better care of them?" His thick eyebrows bristle as he glares at me.

I don't think he's expecting an answer, so I don't say anything. He stomps down the hall.

"What's that about?" I ask Sasha. "I honestly thought he was going to help me."

"He is. He has to climb on the roof from inside the school. Let's wait for him outside."

We dash back to the yard. Recess is almost over and I'm desperate to get the hat back. The bell rings and people join the line to go back to class.

"Should we go in?" I ask.

"Give Gary another minute. He'll be here soon."

We watch as the first of the students walk inside. I'm ready to give up and suggest that we join the line, when I finally see Gary's face over the edge of the roof. I gasp as he squats, glowers at me and tosses the smelly cap down. "Th-thanks," I stutter.

"Are you okay?" Sasha asks me. "You look like you saw a ghost."

Gary is still perched on the edge of the roof, scowling at us.

"Not a ghost," I say. "I always thought there was something different about Gary. Now I know what it is — he's a gargoyle."

Sasha shivers. "You may be right. Let's get out of here before he swoops down on us."

As we make our way back into the school, I decide to forget about carrying the charms around for luck. Losing a good luck charm must be worse than not having one at all, so I have to keep them safely in my locker. And we have instrumental music next period. Today's the day we find out what instrument we're playing and then we sign it out. My arms will be full enough without having to protect my things from Jarrett.

I've been dying to play an instrument since Mary got the flute when she was in grade six. When we made our choices, I took flute as my first pick. Mary would be super-annoyed if I played the same instrument as her, which is the best reason I can think of to play the flute.

When we get to music class, Ms. Martinez reads out the list: "The following students will play the flute: Sasha Kovalik . . . "

I give Sasha a thumbs-up. Wouldn't it be amazing if we were on the same instrument?

" . . . Melissa Gardiner, Alice Woolner, Lily Li, and Lauren Murray. Girls, come to the front and I'll assign you each a flute."

Five girls are standing at the front of the class waiting to receive their flutes, and none of them are me. My stomach sinks. I won't be sitting next to Sasha in band this year. I won't be following Mary around the house practising the flute, like the Pied Piper trying to drive her sister out of the house. The flute was the only instrument I wanted, so I can't even remember what my second and third choices were.

Ms. Martinez reads out the list of clarinets, and I'm not on that either. By the time she begins the trombones, I'm fidgeting in my chair.

"The following people will play trombone: Maggie Ito . . . "

That might be okay. I love the sound of a trombone. Maybe the good luck charms worked. And maybe playing the trombone is what I'll be best at.

" . . . Lionel Chao, Anthony Scott, Jarrett Johnson. Please come forward to receive your instruments."

I can't move. It's as if I've been glued to my chair and will be stuck here for the rest of my life. That would be better than sitting in the same band section as Jarrett.

Sasha catches my eye and throws me a sympathetic glance. That's nice, but what can she do? She's surrounded by a bunch of friendly, well-behaved, reasonable girls. I'm on the same instrument as three boys, including my worst enemy in the world.

"Maggie, can you join us at the front, please?" Ms. Martinez says. The guys are already up there,

Jarrett poking Lionel in the back. It's going to be a long year.

Ms. Martinez hands me my trombone case. It's way heavier than a flute. Carrying a trombone back and forth to practise at home is going to be painful.

"Maggie, I'll ask you to sit on the edge of the row. Jarrett, can you sit next to her? Lionel and Anthony can take the next two spots."

By this time, I'm not surprised by anything that resembles bad luck. Jarrett takes his seat next to me, shoves his fist under his armpit and squeezes. Everyone giggles and Ms. Martinez raises her head from the list of French horns. She can't tell who did it. The three guys are laughing as if Jarrett's done something brilliant.

"That's enough out of the trombone section," she says, lumping me in with them.

As she goes back to her list, I know two things for sure. First: I'm going to hear a lot of bathroom humour this year. And second: the good luck charms didn't work.

5

Dear Maggie,

You must be relieved to have your bandage off.
Just in time to start playing your new instrument.
Your father's rally cap is quite remarkable.
Does it bring his team good luck?
Mrs. Fedorchuk

Dear Mrs. Fedorchuk,

I don't know about his team, but it brought him
good luck once. He caught a foul ball with the cap
at a Jays' game. Too bad it didn't work for me.
Maggie

A week has gone by, and I still haven't figured out
how to lose the curse. On Saturday morning, I meet
Sasha at her place to walk up to Bloor Street. Mom
asked me to buy some buns for lunch, and gave me

her Canadian Wildlife Federation cloth bag to carry them in. She has the most hideous collection of cloth bags I've ever seen, and the CWF bag is the only one I'll be caught dead with.

On the way there, Sasha tells me about the art class she's taking this term. "I love it," she says. "It's about cartooning. I've learned a lot!"

"It sounds great. If I were as good at art as you, I'd take it too."

"You shouldn't worry about it. Lots of kids in the class haven't drawn before, except in school. It's a ton of fun."

"Having fun is one thing. But I want to be best at something. What should I try?"

"They're holding auditions for the school musical next week," Sasha says. "Why don't you try out?"

I was thinking about auditioning, but I wasn't sure I had the nerve. It would be hard to sing in front of the teachers who make the casting decisions. But the idea of being Dorothy in *The Wizard of Oz* is thrilling. If I had the lead role, everyone would know I was the best actress.

"I'll do it!" I say.

We cross the street at Runnymede Road and walk into the Hot Oven bakery. I love the smell of bread that blasts out when we open the door. Along the wall are loaves of sourdough, rye, whole wheat, and white bread. On the bottom shelves are the buns: I choose cheese buns for Mary and me, and olive buns for Mom and Dad. And I pick the biggest croissant for Sasha and me to split. They all go into the CWF bag.

I love croissants, and no one makes them better than Hot Oven. Charlie can keep his chocolate factory — I want my own croissant bakery.

Sasha and I stand in line. It's busy on Saturday mornings while people buy bread for the weekend. We're back almost as far as the front entrance.

The door opens, and Sasha and I squish out of the way to let someone in. I peek as they brush past me and I gasp.

"That's her!" I whisper to Sasha. "The witch!"

The witch has moved toward the back of the store, but her face is reflected in the wall mirror. Sasha frowns. "She doesn't look like a witch to me. Witches have warts, right? And green skin?"

"That's just in *The Wizard of Oz*. If you were a

witch today and wanted to update your style, wouldn't you dress exactly like her?"

"I guess so," Sasha says. She doesn't seem convinced. "You know how we can tell if she's a witch?" she says.

"How?"

"Pour water on her. If she melts, she's definitely a witch."

We're up at the main counter, and I pull out the money to pay for the bread. "Good idea," I say, "but not in here."

As we walk away from the counter, the witch is still browsing at the display. What's she looking at — the gingerbread men?

"Don't touch her," I say. "Pretend you haven't seen her. You don't want to risk this curse."

Once we're out of the bakery, we walk over to the library and sit in the dragon sanctuary. We sit down on the swings and I open the shopping bag. Sasha says, "Speaking of the curse, have you thought of anything else to get rid of it?"

"Yeah," I say. "I was close last time. But I need to do the opposite of what I did before." I split the croissant carefully, making sure that we don't lose any of the flakes. I bite into mine and taste the warm, rich dough.

"You mean bad luck charms?" Sasha asks, brushing the flakes off her shirt.

"Exactly! If I meet the curse head on with bad luck, I'll scare it off."

"How would you do that?"

"The unluckiest thing I can think of is a black cat. We *own* a black cat. So what's the unluckiest thing I could do with her?"

"Probably try to give her a bath."

"True, but I'd rather go with an idea that won't soak the house. You know, walking under a ladder is bad luck."

"Right."

"I'm going to walk under a ladder carrying Neko. Two sets of bad luck will reverse each other, and my life will be great again."

"How do you think of these things?" Sasha says.

I can't do anything else about it this weekend. I'm going to visit my grandma this afternoon, and Sasha can't come over on Sunday. Monday is our first chance to try it out.

When the time comes, Sasha and I talk about the plan on the way to my place after school. The only problem will be keeping Dad inside. He won't understand why I'm skipping homework to drag a ladder and a cat into the driveway. But when we walk into the kitchen, there's a note on the counter. "Mary has an extra piano lesson tonight," it says. "We'll be back by 5:00." It's too good to be true.

"Let's go for it," I say. "Hopefully, I'll be basking in good luck by the time Dad gets home."

We head out to the garage. "Be careful of your arm," Sasha says. "You don't want to hurt it again."

"I'm not *that* unlucky," I say.

I throw open the garage door. The ladder is hanging along the side wall in clear view. Sasha takes one end, I take the other, and we haul it out to the driveway.

We set the ladder up in front of the garage. "Now I have to find Neko," I say. "Unless — maybe I need one more superstition. Bad luck comes in threes. We have the ladder, the black cat — what else can we use?"

"Breaking a mirror is bad luck."

She's right. But I don't want to do anything that

might hurt Neko. "Grandma says it's bad luck to stand my chopsticks straight up and down in my rice," I say.

"We don't have time to make rice," Sasha says. "How about spilling salt? If you spill salt, you're supposed to toss some over your left shoulder or you'll have bad luck."

"Great idea!" I'm ready to go inside for the salt shaker, when I remember the bag of road salt sitting inside the garage. "Perfect," I say, hoisting the half-full bag in my arm. "All this salt has to be way more unlucky than a little shaker."

Which is why, five minutes later, I'm standing beside the ladder in the driveway, Neko in one arm and a bag of road salt in the other. The bag is heavier than I expected, and I shift its weight in my hand.

I dip my head to walk under the ladder and dump a pile of salt on the driveway when I get through. And I stand there with Neko under my arm, and salt all over the ground . . .

Oddly, I don't feel any luckier.

"Should I do it again?"

"Try three times," Sasha suggests. "Since you're doing things in sets of three."

I turn around, duck my head, and walk under the ladder again. My arms are getting tired, and Neko is starting to wriggle. I'm grateful that bad luck doesn't come in sets of seven.

"One more time." I take a deep breath. Another pass and my bad luck will be gone forever. As I duck under the ladder my neighbour with the Chihuahua strolls by. She stops to wave at us. "Hello, girls," she calls.

"Hi, Mrs. Blum," I say, trying to shield Neko so she won't see Princess.

Neko isn't afraid of most dogs, but she's terrified of Princess. The dog barks, and Neko freezes in my arms. Sensing fear, Princess strains at her leash, barking harder.

I feel Neko's claws dig into my arm. I scream and she springs out of my grasp, leaping to the top of the ladder.

"Come on, Princess," says Mrs. Blum, dragging the tiny dog away. Sasha and I fix our gaze on Neko, who is shivering on the top step of the ladder. "Can you coax her down?" Sasha asks.

When Neko is scared, she gets stubborn. I try calling her name. I go in the house and carry out her cat dish. She doesn't budge. I bring her catnip and wave it under her nose. She won't have anything to do with it.

Finally I say, "I have to go and bring her down."

"Are you sure about that?" Sasha asks. "It sounds dangerous, carrying a cat on a ladder."

"I'll be careful."

I don't love ladders, and I feel a little shaky after I leave the second step. I remind myself that I'm doing this to help Neko. And to switch my luck around.

I'm on the fourth step, and I can barely reach Neko if I extend my arm. I stretch — and Neko leaps away from me. I grasp for her on the way down. I miss, and the momentum carries me off the ladder. I tumble to the ground.

"Don't worry," Sasha calls, sprinting toward the garage. "I'll get her."

Just then a car pulls into the driveway. Dad's home. As he and Mary jump out of the car, I survey the scene — Sasha climbing on the barbecue in the garage to grab Neko, me sprawled at the base of the ladder, mountains of salt spilled on the driveway.

"Smooth," Mary says on her way into the house.

"I thought you were doing homework," Dad says.

"We were taking a break," I say. I push myself into a sitting position. I'm covered in cat scratches, and my left arm is throbbing.

There's silence for a minute, as Dad tries to take it in. "You'll be cleaning this up, of course."

"Of course," I say, clutching my arm.

"I've got her!" Sasha shouts, jumping off the barbecue and carrying Neko into the house.

"Tell me again why you were climbing that ladder?" Dad asks.

"I don't know."

I swear it's the truth. I could get into a complicated story about curses and tattoo parlours and chicken legs, but I'm honestly not sure how I ended up outside with a ladder, a cat, and a bag of road salt.

6

Dear Maggie,

I was sorry to see you wearing a tensor bandage again. But I'm confused - wasn't it on your right arm last time?
Mrs. Fedorchuk

Dear Mrs. Fedorchuk,

I sprained my arm last night, but this time it was my left arm. It's going to be hard because I do everything with my left hand. I'm going to photo-copy Sasha's notes this week. I can still play the trombone, but she'll carry it to class for me.

Trying to get rid of the curse is causing its own bad luck. I've decided I need some advice from a real expert. Tonight, I'm going to ask my dad.
Maggie

At the end of the school day, an announcement blasts over the intercom. "Any students who are interested in trying out for *The Wizard of Oz* musical should meet in the gym at 3:30."

"Are you going?" Sasha asks.

"I'm going to give it a try."

"I wish I could wait for you, but I have to go right home," Sasha says. "Call me later and tell me everything."

When I get to the gym, I can't believe how many people are here. Tryouts are open to students in grade six, seven, and eight, so at least there aren't any little kids running around. But it also means I'm competing mostly against older kids.

I see Alice in the gym and sit down beside her. "What role are you trying out for?" I say.

"Dorothy."

"Me, too." We both laugh.

"I wonder who'll try out for the witch," Alice says.

I know someone who'd make a perfect witch, but she doesn't go to school anymore.

Mr. Trevor, the vocal teacher, stands at the front of the gym and tells us when the tryouts are and what we'll do. "On your way out, please pick up a piece of music and script for the role you're interested in. For example, if you're trying out for Dorothy, you'll need two pages of 'Somewhere over the Rainbow' to memorize and sing at the audition." There's a murmur of excitement. Mr. Trevor waits until it dies down and adds, "You will also get two pages of script. Memorize Dorothy's lines, and you'll present those at the audition too."

He points to the table by the door. "Copies of the script and music are available there. And sign-up sheets are on the wall. No running, please. There are more than enough spots."

As we leave, Alice and I stop at the sign-up sheets. Tryouts begin a week from today.

"Let's audition back-to-back," she says. She takes out a pen. "How about next Thursday before school?"

"Sure!" I laugh. "Can you sign my time slot for me? I can't use my left hand, and my right hand writes like a five year old."

At my locker, I flip through the forms I picked up. The script doesn't seem like much to memorize. Maybe the tryouts won't be hard after all.

I imagine myself on stage, wearing Dorothy's blue gingham dress and ponytails. As I say "Auntie Em, there's no place like home," the school gym erupts into cheers. In my imagination, I take my bow and scoop up the bouquets my friends have tossed onto the stage. All I have to do is win the audition.

Mary has band practice tonight, so it'll be just Dad and me for a while. That's why tonight is a good time to ask him for advice. I need to be careful what I say, because I don't want to mention the tattoo shop or the curse. But none of my ideas are working. I can use some help. Nobody has better ideas than Dad.

When I walk into the house, Dad's kneeling on the kitchen floor next to the cabinet door under the sink. He waves at me. "I'm going to Canadian Tire to buy a hinge for this door. Do you want to come?"

"I'm in!" I say. Dad loves Canadian Tire and, if he isn't distracted, I'll ask his opinion while we're there.

We jump in the car and Dad backs out into the street. On our way, we drive past Fresh Ink. I try not to stare, but I can't help it. Luckily Dad's too busy steering around the double-parked van to notice what I'm looking at. The car ahead of us honks and traffic comes to a stop.

The building is creepier this time. The cement planters are choked with orange and yellow blooms. I see the messy carpet of maple leaves and stray petals that lie thick on the lawn and the sidewalk leading to the front door.

I wonder if the witch is in there — and if not, I wonder where she is. Running into her somewhere other than the haunted house seems worse than seeing her there. It means I could be anywhere — bakery, fruit shop, even the library — and she might show up. But I'm not worried about seeing her at Canadian Tire. Witches and hardware don't mix.

We squeeze around the van and Dad drives to Canadian Tire. When we get there, he marches to the back of the store with me trailing behind. I follow him to aisle 57.

While Dad scans the different sizes and varieties of hinges, I decide it's a good time to ask.

"Dad, if you wanted to turn your luck around, what would you do?"

"Why do you have to turn your luck around?" he asks, not taking his eyes off the shelves.

"Everything I do gets messed up."

"Give me an example." Dad reaches for two competing styles of hinges. He flips them over to read about their features.

"In band I asked to play the flute, and I got trombone. Which is okay, but Jarrett's on trombone, too."

Dad smiles. "Is that bad luck?"

"It's terrible luck! He bugs me all the time." I hesitate, but Dad has to understand how terrible this curse is. "I switched our locks the other day, and Mrs. Fedorchuk caught me." I don't mention about Jarrett stealing the smelly cap. Now that it's back in Dad's closet, he doesn't need to know how close it came to ending its life on the school roof.

"Sounds like your bad luck is related to Jarrett Johnson. I wonder if befriending your enemy is the answer."

My voice goes up about an octave. "You think I should be nice to Jarrett?!"

"You want to break a pattern, right?"

I pretend to scan the hinges on the wall. "I don't know what you mean." I'm hoping for an idea that isn't going to be so disgusting. Like wearing the smelly cap for the rest of my life.

Dad hangs one of the hinges back on its hook and we head up to the front counter with the other one. As the cashier rings us through, Dad asks, "How long have you hated Jarrett?"

"Since I was born."

"I'd call that a pattern. Why don't you try to be as nice as you can, and see if that changes your luck?"

Yuck, I think. "For how long?"

"Try a day."

"A whole day? Being nice to Jarrett for a day would be worse than fending off a pack of Dementors."

Dad pockets his change and ten cents in Canadian Tire money. "Just one day. And it has to be a school day. If it doesn't work, you can go back to your usual relationship twenty-four hours later."

I consider it on the way home. It's the worst thing I can imagine, but maybe Dad's right. I need a drastic change, and being friends with Jarrett would definitely be drastic. I'll give it a shot.

As soon as I get home, I call Sasha. "How did the meeting go?" she asks.

"Okay. A lot of people are trying out for Dorothy."

"You'll be awesome!"

"I hope so. I only have a week to learn the music and the lines."

"You don't sound very excited," Sasha says.

"I'm excited about the musical. What I'm not excited about is the advice Dad gave me."

"What did he say?"

"That I should try getting along with Jarrett for a day, and it might improve my luck."

Sasha giggles. "Is he serious? You're not actually going to try it, are you?"

"I don't have a choice. Unless you have any other ideas?"

She doesn't. I guess tomorrow I'm making a new friend. But I wonder if the cure for the curse is worse than the curse itself.

7

Dear Maggie,

I was pleased to hear that you're trying out for a role in *The Wizard of Oz*. You're so dramatic - you'll do a great job!

Only a few students from grade six are auditioning for a role, and five of them are from my class. Good thing you get the bandage off in a few more days - Dorothy needs both arms to fend off that witch!
Mrs. Fedorchuk

Dear Mrs. Fedorchuk,

I'm excited too! I'm not sure about the singing, but I love to act. The scene that I'm doing for the audition is when the Wicked Witch of the West tries to steal Toto from Dorothy. It's very thrilling! (It also reminds me of Jarrett trying to steal my stuff.)
Maggie

Project "Be Nice to Jarrett" gets off to a good start because we have vocal music first period and, unlike in instrumental, Jarrett and I sit at opposite ends of the class. All I need to do is have positive thoughts about him. Or not think about him at all. How hard can that be?

The principal comes to the door of the music room and waves to Mr. Trevor to come out. "I can hear everything that goes on," Mr. Trevor says, before he steps into the hall. "No silly stuff. I'll be back in one minute."

I completely ignore Jarrett as I talk to Sasha. At least, I try to ignore him. I can hear him fooling around with Lionel on the other side of the class.

"You wouldn't believe what those guys are doing," Sasha says.

I sneak a look. They're balancing on the back legs of their chairs and trying to knock each other off. I turn back. "Doesn't matter. I'm not going to watch."

"Why not?"

"Because I'm trying to have positive thoughts about Jarrett. If I watch what he's doing, I'll think he's a goof."

Sasha frowns toward the other side of the room. "Yeah, you probably will."

I hear a loud crash, and Mr. Trevor rushes in. Jarrett and his chair are lying sideways on the floor.

"Get up," Mr. Trevor sighs. "Can't I take my eyes off you for a minute?"

It would be easier to have positive thoughts about Jarrett if we didn't have to be in the same room.

The real challenge comes next period in instrumental. No possibility of ignoring him here. Sasha squeezes my arm on the way in. "Good luck," she whispers. "If you can be nice to him in band, you deserve the best luck ever."

I slide into my chair and smile at Jarrett.

"Hey, fish breath," he says.

"Hi, Jarrett," I say. I feel like vomiting. I remind myself that it's for a good cause. "You sound great on the trombone. Have you been practising a lot?" I can hardly choke the words out of my mouth. He hasn't taken the trombone home once.

Jarrett stares at me like I've just floated in from Kansas in a flying house. He turns in the other direction and pokes Lionel. Not a great start, but at least neither of us is lying sideways on the floor.

Jarrett and I share a music stand. I force myself to be pleasant and set the score for "Hot Cross Buns" on his side of the stand so it's easier for him to read. Ms. Martinez begins to conduct. About two bars in, Lionel reaches out and snatches our sheet music. He sticks it in the trombone case under his chair. Jarrett responds by grabbing the music from Lionel and Anthony's stand and sitting on it.

"Put it up on *our* stand," I whisper. Jarrett ignores me. And with one good arm, I can barely play the trombone, let alone fight somebody for a piece of music. So the entire section mimes playing the rest of the song. Ms. Martinez glares at us but keeps conducting.

After the band limps through "Hot Cross Buns," Ms. Martinez says, "I couldn't hear the trombone section. I want each of you to play the first two lines of music so I can be sure you're getting it."

This might be a problem, with one piece of music under Jarrett's bum and the other under Lionel's chair. Finally, Jarrett stands up and reaches for the music. I assume he's going to put it up on the stand — but that would be way too easy.

He flips over to the second page and sits back on it, as if he's reading it with his butt.

All the guys behind us in percussion burst out laughing. Ms. Martinez presses her lips together tightly.

"*You* may be able to read the music from there, but Maggie can't," she says. "Set it back on the stand."

Now everyone in the class is laughing. Mission accomplished, Jarrett sets the music back on the stand.

"Maggie, please lead us off," Ms. Martinez says.

I lift the mouthpiece to my lips. I've been practising every night, so it shouldn't be too hard. Jarrett leans forward and begins counting the time. The only problem is, he's counting in 3/4 and the music is in 4/4. I play about three bars before I completely lose my rhythm.

"That's enough, Maggie," she says. "Your tone is excellent, but you need to spend more time practising the timing."

That is so unfair! And the worst part is, I can't mess up Jarrett's counting or kick him. So even though he never practises, his playing sounds better than mine.

When class lets out, I'm fuming. Most of the flute section comes over to console me.

"I saw what Jarrett was doing," Alice says. "I can't believe Ms. Martinez didn't notice."

"All it proves," Sasha says, "is that trying to be his friend isn't working. At least you can go back to ignoring him and teasing him back."

"My dad said I should try for a whole day," I say glumly. Right then Lionel walks by. I hope he didn't hear what I said. If Jarrett finds out that I *have* to be nice to him, things might get even worse.

Nobody says anything else. There's nothing else to say. Being friendly with Jarrett for a day is more than any of us can imagine.

Thank goodness Sasha and I come back to my place for lunch. At least it gives me a break from Project "Be Nice to Jarrett".

Sasha helps me practise my *Wizard Of Oz* lines at lunch. We get so preoccupied that we lose track of time and we have to run to get back to school.

We stop at the office to pick up late slips. And now I have to sit through a double class of Being Nice to Jarrett, formerly known as English. In homeroom,

Jarrett still sits at the table next to mine, so I can just see him out of the corner of my eye. When I glance over to see what he's up to, he bats his eyelashes at me. I pivot toward the front of the class, determined to ignore him again.

He reaches across the aisle and grabs my lip gloss. My left arm is still in the bandage, and I'm not fast enough to reach it with my right.

"Stop that!" I whisper. "Give it back!"

"You're not being very *nice* to me," he whines. He checks the front of the room to make sure that Mrs. Fedorchuk is busy at her desk answering Lauren's question, then he pulls the lid off the lip gloss and pretends to apply it.

He is so gross. He makes kissy-lips at Anthony. I shake my head and try to focus on my work.

A couple of minutes later, Jarrett brushes past me on his way to the pencil sharpener. I move everything valuable to where he can't reach it, but he doesn't take anything. I guess the lip gloss was what he really wanted.

Soon there's a lot of giggling behind me. I spin around, but don't see anything funny. I face the front, and once again people start laughing.

Both Lauren and Mrs. Fedorchuk hear the noise and lift their heads.

"Please keep the noise down," Mrs. Fedorchuk says. "Independent work time is a privilege you receive only when you earn it. I'd like you to be coming up with ideas for your creative writing project."

I still hear stifled giggles. Alice comes from the back of the class and bends down beside me. "Jarrett hung something on the back of your chair when he walked by. You might want to take it down."

I spin and rip off the blue sheet of paper. It reads: "Magnolia needs watering."

"This is war!" I whisper to Sasha.

"But you're being nice to him — "

"The war starts tomorrow!"

Alice leans in. "There's something else I have to tell you."

Mrs. Fedorchuk looks up again. "There's a lot of commotion today. Alice, please take your seat. And Jarrett, unless you're interested in a modeling career, please return Maggie's lip gloss."

The class bursts into laughter. Jarrett is so embarrassed when he hands it back that I almost feel sorry for him. Almost.

In fact, I enjoy his humiliation so much that I forget about Alice's last words until recess. She and Lauren race over to talk to Sasha and me the minute we hit the schoolyard.

"Bad news," Lauren says. "Jarrett heard about what you're doing."

"Rats! Lionel must have heard us talking."

"I heard him saying he's going to be mean on purpose today, because you can't do anything back."

"That's the worst news you could give me," I fume.

She and Alice exchange glances. "Actually, it isn't," Alice says.

I look at her, puzzled. Just then, Lionel runs out of the school, laughing. "Hi, Maggot," he says, and dashes away.

More giggling from beside us in the playground. I spin, and Nathaniel and Annica are standing there. Nathaniel grins. "Hi Maggot!" he says.

I shake my head. "What's going on?"

"Don't kill us," Lauren says.

"I won't kill you. What's up?"

"Some of the kids are saying you and Jarrett are a couple."

"WHAT!?"

"They think you like him because you're being nice to him," Alice says. "So they sandwiched your names together, like a mashup name. They're calling you and Jarrett 'Maggot.'"

I groan. "How many people know?"

"Everyone was talking about it at lunch."

I close my eyes. I wish I was dead. No, I wish Jarrett was dead. "This is a disaster. My life is worse than before."

"If it makes you feel better, he hates it too," Lauren says. "That's why he called you Magnolia in class. He wants people to forget about Maggot."

"Incredible!" I say. "Jarrett and I actually agree on something."

Who'd guess I'd find a name I hate more than Magnolia?

But it gives me an idea. If having a mashup name bugs Jarrett, maybe I've found the way to get to him. Pretending I *want* to be his girlfriend would drive him nuts!

At least there's one bit of good news: being nice to Jarrett didn't get rid of the curse, so I'm off the hook.

8

Dear Maggie,

    I see your tensor bandage is off again. Hooray! Good luck in the tryout for the musical. I'd love to see you do some acting in the classroom. Perhaps you could act out one of your class presentations this year.

    By the way, I've seen that Jarrett has been teasing you a lot lately. You've been very mature by not retaliating.

Mrs. Fedorchuk

Dear Mrs. Fedorchuk,

    I'm trying to ignore Jarrett. Some days that's easier than others.

Maggie

I can ignore Jarrett for now. After all, I need to devote my attention to the tryout. But once that's done,

I'm moving on to Project Romance.

Later that week, I'm at home rehearsing my *Wizard of Oz* dialogue out loud when Mary walks in. "You sound good," she says, "but you'd sound better if you had a witch to practise with."

What's she up to? Did she find out what happened on Bloor Street? Is she making fun of me?

She laughs. "I'm serious. If you want me to practise with you, I will. I make a great witch."

I can't believe she's offering to help me. Is this the week everyone is being nice to their enemies? Whatever her reason, I hand her the script.

She has the first line. "What a nice little dog! And you, my dear. What an unexpected pleasure! It's so kind of you to visit me in my loneliness."

Mary's witch voice is so creepy that she gives me goose bumps. I close my eyes and imagine that somebody is hurting Neko. I love my cat as much as Dorothy loves her dog.

"What are you going to do with my dog?" I say — and I actually feel a tingle of panic. "Give him back to me!"

Mary responds, "All in good time, my little pretty —

70

all in good time."

I wish she wasn't enjoying this so much. I plead, "Oh, please give me back my dog!"

When we're done the lines, Mary says, "You're not half bad. You'd make a good Dorothy." Then she cackles, reminding me that she could turn back into a witch at any time.

"Thanks," I say.

"Have you been working on the song, too?" she asks.

"A couple of times, I guess." I sing the first verse for her:

"Somewhere over the rainbow
Way up high
There's a land that I heard of
Once in a lullaby."

"That's pretty boring," Mary says. "It would be way funnier if you sang it like this:

"Somewhere over the rainbow
Boys are smart.
Jarrett tried out for Tin Man
Perfect — he has no heart."

I burst out laughing. "Awesome!" I shout. She's

71

funny, but I also love that I'm in on the joke. With Mary, usually I'm the one being laughed at.

"Keep practising the song," she says, grabbing her backpack on her way out of the room. "You've got the lines down, but you need to sing well, too."

Singing "Somewhere over the Rainbow" isn't as much fun as practising the script, but I run through it a few times every day. Sometimes I use Mary's words, just for fun.

On the day of my tryout, I arrive five minutes early. I peek through the classroom window and see Alice at the front singing for the teachers. They're facing her, sitting in the kids' seats in the classroom, and some of them are taking notes. Every teacher in the school must be there. Alice's voice filters through the door, and she sounds amazing. I swallow hard. What am I doing here?

When Alice finishes singing, she comes out of the class smiling. Mr. Trevor walks her to the door and says, "We'll call you in a couple of minutes, Maggie." He shuts the door behind her.

"They did the same thing at the audition before

mine," Alice says. "I was already nervous, but that made it ten times worse. It felt like I sat outside the class for hours until they called me in. The longer they talk about you, the better your chances."

"How did you do?" I ask.

"Pretty good. My voice teacher gave me lots of tips."

I forgot that Alice takes voice lessons. Why didn't I spend more time practising the song?

Alice continues. "Between her suggestions at my lesson and the practising I did, I was ready. Did you bring a pitch pipe?"

"What?"

"A pitch pipe. There isn't a piano in the class, so you need a pitch pipe to give you a starting note." She sees my frown. "Do you want to borrow mine?"

"Uh, no thanks." I don't know what my starting note is.

The door opens. "Maggie, we're ready for you."

"Good luck," Alice says.

I shuffle in and walk to the front of the class. There are at least eight teachers in the room, and every one of them is facing me. This is almost as bad as walking into a haunted house.

My mind goes blank. I can't remember any of my lines.

"Let's begin with the script," Ms. Martinez says. "You're Dorothy, and I'll be the witch."

I take a deep breath, and pretend I'm in the living room again with Mary. I remember what it's like to feel as if I'm Dorothy and Neko is being threatened. The further I get into the script, the more I relate to her. I actually feel myself shaking as I say, "No! No — no! Here, — you can have your old slippers, — but give me back Toto."

A couple of teachers jot notes in their clipboards and they're both smiling. *My luck is changing*, I think.

"Great job, Maggie. And now, please sing for us," Mr. Trevor says.

Alice was right about no piano. And obviously I don't have a pitch pipe. I struggle to remember where I started when I sang the song at home. I have no idea. I choose a random note.

"Some — where . . . " way too high. My voice cracks badly on "where." I stop. "Can I try again?" I ask.

"Of course," Mr. Trevor says.

I start a few notes lower. Still a bit high, but at least my voice isn't cracking:

"Somewhere over the rainbow,

Boys are smart.

Jarrett tried out for Tin Man

Perfect — he has no heart."

I stop singing. Did I really do that, or am I dreaming? From the look on Mr. Trevor's face, it's no dream. Now I know how Jarrett must have felt when he got caught with my lip gloss.

Nobody says anything about the words I messed up. Also, none of the teachers write in their clipboards the whole time.

Ms. Martinez stands up. "Thank you for trying out, Maggie." She shuts the door behind me. At least I don't hear laughter coming from the classroom.

Naturally, my worst enemy is sitting outside the door — and guess what? He's got a pitch pipe in his hand. If he heard me singing, I will just die. "Break a leg," I say to Jarrett.

"You too. Then you could wear your bandage again."

Why is Jarrett always a step ahead of me? I try to think of a comeback, but the door opens. "Jarrett, you're on."

They didn't need fifteen minutes to discuss my audition. If there was any doubt before, it's gone: I am definitely cursed.

9

Dear Maggie,

   I see that you're being unusually friendly to Jarrett this week. I wonder if that's because you want to be buddies, or because it gets under his skin?

   Please thank your dad for the cookies he sent in last week. They were delicious! Do you ever cook with him?

Mrs. Fedorchuk

Dear Mrs. Fedorchuk,

   I don't cook with my dad very often, but I should start. He's good at it, and maybe I will be, too.

Maggie

I've been thinking about Mrs. Fedorchuk's e-mail since I read it this morning. I'd love to be best at cooking. Hot Oven's croissants are delicious, and it's something that Dad never bakes. I can't think of a better way to banish this curse than by cooking my way out of it.

After school I race home, determined to make croissants for dinner. I pull a few cookbooks out of the cupboard and search for a recipe. There are recipes for crepes and cranberry muffins and even crab cakes, but no croissants.

Dad walks into the kitchen. "What're you doing with the cookbooks, Mags?" he asks.

"I'd like to make dinner tonight."

"Great! What do you have in mind?"

"Croissants."

Dad frowns. "Croissants are pretty difficult. And they take a long time to make. You wouldn't finish them by dinner. But you could try something that's faster to make. How about macaroni and cheese?"

I wrinkle my nose. "Anyone can make Kraft Dinner. I don't want to cook something that comes out of a box."

"No, I mean real macaroni and cheese. With a creamy homemade cheese sauce that makes you want to lick your plate."

Hearing him talk about it makes my mouth water. And macaroni and cheese is better for dinner than croissants, anyway.

"Sounds great!" I say. As Dad reaches for the cookbook, I imagine myself whipping up fantastic meals, opening a restaurant, even getting my own TV cooking show. Maybe someday Dad will pull one of my cookbooks out of the cupboard!

"I'll help you with the cheese sauce," he says. "You can make a salad while the pasta's in the oven."

We melt the butter in a pot and add some flour.

"This is the tough part," Dad says. "Once you add the milk, you have to keep stirring until it's smooth and thick. You can't wander away and work on other things or the sauce will go lumpy. Maybe even burn."

"I won't leave the stove until you tell me to," I say.

I add the milk and stir like crazy.

"Not too fast," Dad says. "Just slow and steady."

I settle into a gentle rhythm, and Dad grates the cheese while I stir.

"Did you try being nice to Jarrett yet?" he asks.

I make a face. "I tried."

Dad laughs. "Oops. That bad?"

"The worst. He found out what I was doing. Then he was extra-mean on purpose because I couldn't be mean back."

"Sounds as if I gave you the wrong suggestion. I'm sorry it didn't help."

"That's okay," I say. "Jarrett messes everyone up."

I watch as the sauce begins to thicken. I imagine myself triumphantly serving homemade mac and cheese to Sasha on a silver tray. "Hey Dad," I say. "Can I make this the next time Sasha comes over? And do we own a silver tray?"

Dad laughs. "No to the tray, but yes to the dinner." The phone rings and he sets down the grater to pick it up. "Hello," he says. Pause. "Really? Already?" He glances at me. "I think so. Hang on a minute."

He holds the receiver to the side and says, "That's Mary. Her band practice is over early. I need to pick her up and I've promised to drive a couple of her friends home. Are you okay here, or should I ask them to wait a while?"

I'm tempted to let Mary sit and wait, but I remember

how she helped me with my lines. I also want to finish making dinner by myself. "I'm okay," I say.

When Dad hangs up he says, "Give the sauce another couple of minutes then add the cheese and stir until it melts. Do you feel comfortable finishing the pasta and the salad on your own?"

I nod.

"Let me turn on the oven before I go," Dad says.

"Dad, I'm not a baby."

He smiles and pulls his hand back from the oven knob. "Of course you're not. Mary and I will be back in about forty-five minutes. You can serve dinner anytime after that."

When he leaves, I turn on the oven and stir the sauce another minute. I lift the spoon in the air and let the sauce drip off. It's thick and creamy, like Dad promised, and I take it off the burner to add the cheese. It melts as I stir, and it smells delicious.

The rest of the meal is easy. I combine the sauce with the macaroni and set it in the oven. I wash the lettuce and mix it with diced carrots and peppers. The croutons and dressings go on the table.

I'm done so quickly that I decide to make dessert,

too. There isn't time for cake, but I can whip up a batch of chocolate chip cookies.

I find Dad's Bonnie Stern cookbook, which automatically opens to chocolate chip cookies. He's made these so many times he practically has the recipe memorized.

It doesn't take long to make the cookie dough. It looks delicious, though the batter seems gooier than Dad's usually does. I set the shaped cookies beside the stove to wait until the mac and cheese is cooked.

By the time Dad and Mary get home, I'm taking the casserole out of the oven. "You can sit down," I say. "Dinner's nearly ready!" The cookies go in the oven to bake while we're eating. I serve the macaroni and cheese onto three plates and arrange the salads beside. I carry the plates to the dining room table.

"Bon appétit!" Dad says, lifting a forkful of mac and cheese to his mouth. There's a crunching sound, and Dad looks puzzled. I bring a forkful to my mouth. The cheese sauce tastes delicious on my tongue.

And then I take a bite. It's crispy.

"Uh, Maggie?" Dad asks. "Did you remember to cook the macaroni?"

"You have to cook the macaroni first?"

There's silence around the table. I close my eyes in horror.

"This is a first," Mary says. "If we get tired of talking to each other, we can communicate in Morse Code as we eat." She chews noisily in patterns of dots and dashes.

"You make mistakes too," I say, although I can't think of any. "And we can eat the salad."

Mary makes a face as she reaches for her fork. "Is it possible to mess up lettuce?"

"That's enough, Mary. The salad will be delicious," Dad says. He laughs. "I've had dozens of cooking disasters. Every cook has. Don't let it discourage you, Maggie. That's why I keep peanut butter and jelly in the house."

Peanut butter and jelly sandwiches with salad. Not a bad meal, but not what I planned. Dad makes a big deal about how good the salad is, which is kind of embarrassing. It's what you'd say to a five year old.

When we're done eating I say, "I made dessert, too."

"Good work, Maggie," Dad says. "How did you find the time?"

On my way to the kitchen, I hear Mary muttering, "She found the time by not cooking the macaroni." I wish I'd kept her and her friends waiting at the school.

I pull the cookies out of the oven. Or maybe I should say "cookie," because the batter slid together into one hard rectangle on the cookie sheet.

Mary has come into the kitchen with the dirty dishes, and she laughs. "Looks like the Pillsbury Doughboy had a collision with a steam roller," she says.

"You probably added too much butter," Dad says. "Never mind, we'll try cutting them like brownies." He gives me a hug, but it doesn't make me feel better.

The curse strikes again, and this time it tastes awful.

10

Dear Maggie,

I was sorry to hear that you didn't get a callback for Dorothy, but they'll be casting many other roles. I'll keep my fingers crossed that you win one of those.

Mrs. Fedorchuk

Dear Mrs. Fedorchuk,

I'm crossing my fingers too, but the way my luck is going, I don't think I'll get a break again. Unless it's my arm.

Maggie

After dinner, I read Mrs. Fedorchuk's e-mail and remember the bad things that have happened since the beginning of school, and how I've tried to turn my luck around. It looks as if I'll be cursed for the rest of my life. And part of the curse will be never being best at anything.

I flop down on the living room couch and pick up a book. If I can't be best at anything, maybe I'll spend the rest of my life hanging out.

Just then, Mary wanders into the room, talking on the phone. "I can't believe we have to finish reading it by next week," she says. She's talking homework again. "It's impossible. And we have that quote test next week." I try to block out her whining by humming softly, which I know bugs her.

I'm about to hum a little more loudly, when I tune back in to Mary's side of the conversation. "When the witches say, 'Fair is foul and foul is fair,' it stands for things being the wrong way around," she says.

Witches? Mary believes in witches?

I pretend to read, but I'm not going to miss another word she says.

"It's in Act One. When their first prophecy comes true, Macbeth believes everything else the witches say."

Okay, the witches are just in a story. Mary still might be able to help me.

When she's done on the phone, I set down my book and say, "Tell me about the witches."

She clacks her teeth at me, as if she's talking in Morse Code.

I toss a cushion in her direction. "I'm serious. I want to know."

She tosses the cushion back. "Do you have to eavesdrop on every conversation I have?" But she doesn't look mad. Sometimes she likes talking to me if she can prove how smart she is.

"I thought a story about witches sounded cool," I say.

"It isn't a story, it's a play called *Macbeth*. The witches tell him the things he's going to do and he acts on what they say. He would have been better off not listening to them."

"Does he kill them at the end?" I ask hopefully. "Or get rid of their evil curse?"

"No. He dies." Mary laughs.

That's not what I want to hear. "Did it tell about the curse they put on him?"

Mary hesitates. "Actually, it gives the recipe they used."

A recipe for a curse! Now we're getting somewhere. "What is it?"

"I don't know if it's an actual curse," Mary says. "But it's a stew that has horrible things in it, like a newt's eye and a frog's toe."

Is she making fun of me?

"I'm serious," she says. "Part of it goes:

"Fillet of a fenny snake,

In the cauldron boil and bake:

Eye of newt and toe of frog,

Wool of bat, and tongue of dog —"

This is what they study in high school? Witch cookbooks? Sounds like the kind of book Jarrett would read.

Still, Mary has given me an important clue. I wait until she leaves the room, then do an Internet search for "Macbeth witches quotes." I find a long poem about stuff they added to the stew. The lines Mary quoted are only part of it. Some of the ingredients I don't understand. But it gives me a new idea.

Maybe it takes a witch's recipe to get rid of a witch.

Sasha seems less than enthusiastic when I tell her on Friday night. We just finished eating my delicious macaroni and cheese — I cooked the macaroni this time — and we're sitting cross-legged on my bed. "You haven't got half that stuff," she says. "And the last time you used substitutes they didn't work."

"Yes, but last time I wasn't using a real witch's recipe. This time I'll have a potion I can drink! And the main reason the charms didn't work is because Mrs. Fedorchuk made me keep them in my locker."

"Nothing's worked yet, even though you've tried. You might have to wait until the curse wears off."

"I have a good feeling about this," I say. "I'm going to give it a shot."

"Okay. But when will you do it?"

"Tonight. After Mom and Dad fall asleep, I'll have the kitchen to myself. Want to sleep over and give me a hand?"

Sasha laughs. "Sneaking around in the middle of the night to make a potion isn't my idea of a fun sleepover. But tell me what you're going to do."

I open the bottom drawer of my dresser and remove Mom's Wildlife Federation bag, which is stuffed with supplies. I drag the ingredients out one by one. "A few grapes for newts' eyes," I say.

"I think you should keep those in the fridge," Sasha says. "They're a bit . . . squishy."

"Eyeballs *should* be squishy. I also bought a bag of gummy worms for the fenny snakes. I don't know what a fenny snake is, but hopefully a worm is close enough."

"Sounds delicious. What else?"

"I bought some green jelly beans for the frog's toes. For wool of bat, I took some hair from my hairbrush."

"That's the most disgusting thing I've ever heard of."

"I didn't mention the cat food I'm using for the tongue of dog."

"I'm glad it's you drinking it, and not me," Sasha says, making a face. "How horrible."

"It has to be horrible if it's going to work."

"Do you think it'll get rid of the curse?"

"I hope so."

"If it does, maybe it'll help you get a role in *The Wizard of Oz*. It would be great if you and Alice were both in the musical. At least, if she still wants to." Alice got a callback for Dorothy, but in the end a girl in grade eight got the role instead. "I saw her crying after school," Sasha says.

"I heard some of her audition, and she was great. She'll get a good part."

Sasha hesitates. "I hope it doesn't bug you that Jarrett's the Tin Man."

"I don't care either way," I say. But personally, I'd cast him as a Winged Monkey.

After Sasha goes home, I set the alarm for 2 a.m. and shove it under my pillow. I don't want to risk waking Mom and Dad. Before I crawl into bed, I open my jewelry box and examine the broomstick earring. I wish I hadn't caught it on my sleeve in the first place. But I did, and somehow I have to make up for it.

I barely budge when the alarm goes off. It feels as if I slept about two minutes. I groan, push myself up, eyes half shut, and drag my hand across my forehead. This potion had better be worth it.

I pull out the bag of ingredients and sneak down to the kitchen. The first thing I need to do is make a sauce, like I did with the macaroni. Otherwise, I'm basically drinking grapes and cat food. But instead of adding cheese, I'll put in the eye of newt and toe of frog.

I measure the butter and flour, then add the milk and watch it thicken. I imagine how it's going to taste once it's finished, and my stomach lurches in disgust. But I'm determined: I really want to get rid of this curse.

I open the tin of cat food and spoon about half of it into the sauce. I add the grapes, the jelly beans and the hair. I'm set to dunk the gummy worms when I wonder if worms actually are close enough to snakes for this to work. I wouldn't want to mess up now. So I decide to check what "fenny" means.

I sneak into the living room, careful to avoid tripping on my backpack around the corner. The last thing I want to do is wake Mom and Dad.

I do an Internet search for "fenny," but none of the answers have anything to do with witches. I'm not used to being up this late, and I blink to refocus on the page.

Maybe I misunderstood, and it's really "funny" snakes.

As I type "funny snakes," I sniff the air. Something

smells awful. Like it's burning.

I remember Dad's words to me as I made the original cheese sauce. "You can't wander away and work on other things or the sauce will go lumpy. Maybe even burn."

I leap off the computer chair and run toward the hall. I'm nearly there when I crash into a large lump. My backpack. I manage not to fall on my hands and knees by clutching the door frame to keep on my feet. If only I can make it to the stove before, before —

The smoke alarm goes off.

I've heard it go off during the day, but it's never seemed this loud. When I make it to the kitchen, I see the pot on the stove on high heat. Smoke is billowing out and the sauce is caked and dried on the bottom. I grab a dishtowel and stick the pot under the tap. It hisses and steams, and I back away.

The smoke alarm is still screeching.

I hear the creak of my parents' bed as one, then two bodies scramble out. This is followed by the sound of two sets of footsteps thundering down the stairs. Mom and Dad race into the kitchen in their pajamas, eyes wide open.

Mom dashes to the stove and shuts off the heat. She checks the pot in the sink. Dad flings the kitchen window open, and the cool night air flows in.

The smoke alarm shuts off as suddenly as it began. The silence in the kitchen echoes in my ears, broken only by the sizzling of the pot.

Mary stumbles down the stairs. Now I'm in real trouble. Mom and Dad might lecture me or ground me, but Mary can make my life extremely miserable.

"What's going on?" Mom asks. "This is a very dangerous situation." She folds her arms across her chest. Mary, standing beside her, folds her arms to match Mom's. Mom looks serious, but Mary looks like one of Cinderella's evil stepsisters, if she was going to the ball in her nightgown.

"I was trying to make a sauce," I mumble.

"At two o'clock in the morning?" Dad says. He scratches his head, as if he hopes that eventually it will make sense.

"I know it was stupid," I say. "I'm sorry."

"But why were you cooking in the middle of the night?" Mom asks.

I sigh. "Because I'm an idiot, I guess."

"At least we all agree on that," Mary says.

"Back to bed, Mary," Mom says, pointing upstairs. "You're not being helpful."

Even in my moment of shame, it's strangely pleasant seeing Mary get in trouble when it's me who almost burned down the house. Mary shuffles up and Mom and Dad focus their attention back on me.

"The kitchen needs to be cleaned, and it can't wait until morning," Mom says. "We'll supervise, but you're doing the work."

"Maggie, we simply can't have you doing reckless things like this," Dad adds. "You have to think before you act."

I spend the next twenty minutes wiping the stove and counter, and scrubbing the pot, and listening to Mom and Dad tell me what a huge risk I took and what the consequences will be. For two weeks, I have to come home for lunch every day, and I have to come home right after school. I can't have any friends over. And no cooking by myself. That rule will probably last for two *decades*.

This curse is ruining my life.

When I'm done cleaning and listening to the

lecture, I head back to bed. I lie awake for a long time, thinking about everything that's happened.

I'm ready to give up. I'm out of ideas to get rid of this curse, and I don't want to try anything else. Every single plan has been worse than the one before.

The only other thing I can do is ask for advice from the person who might be my fairy godmother.

It's time to talk to Mrs. Fedorchuk.

11

Dear Mrs. Fedorchuk,
   I know it's your turn to write, but can I talk
to you after school some day this week? I need some
advice.
Maggie

Dear Maggie,
   I'd be happy to talk about whatever is on your
mind. I'm free Monday after school and would love
to see you then.
Mrs. Fedorchuk

It's Monday morning, and on the way to school I give
Sasha a shortened version of what happened.

"This is my last chance," I say. "If Mrs. Fedorchuk
doesn't have any ideas, I'm doomed forever."

"She's smart," Sasha says. "She'll think of something."

"I hope she does. Luckily I saw her e-mail last night and Mom and Dad said it's okay if I see her after school. As long as I come home right afterward."

Sasha and I walk into the schoolyard and there's Jarrett, leaning against the fence, talking to a group of guys.

"I can't start Project Romance with Jarrett," I say. "Not after what happened this weekend."

Sasha looks at me, horrified. "Grounded or not, if you don't, you're letting him win! You can't let that happen!"

I think about that for a minute. "I guess you're right." I force a big smile and we both wander over to where the boys are standing. "Jarrett," I say, "Congratulations on the musical. You'll be a fantastic Tin Man." Then I stop talking and grin at him. Jarrett looks like he wants to sink into the ground—all his friends are there—and the longer I smile, the worse it gets for him. Just knowing how much it bugs him cheers me up a ton.

Lionel bursts out laughing. "Do you want to talk to your girlfriend?" he asks Jarrett.

Jarrett clenches his jaw. "She's not my girlfriend," he says.

Anthony bats his eyelashes. "Because if the two of you want to hang out together, we can give you some privacy."

Sasha and I exchange glances. All I have to do is stand here. The guys are doing my dirty work for me.

Jarrett lunges at Anthony and the two of them start wrestling. I consider calling out, "Go Jarrett, go!" but decide that's over the top, even for Project Romance.

I turn to Sasha to discuss how it's going, when two lumbering bodies bump into me. My feet fly into the air and I hit the ground hard.

"Ow!" I yell.

They stop wrestling and bend over me. "Oh, man," Anthony says. "I hope you're all right."

Jarrett looks as if he'd rather be eating insects than asking about my health, but he grunts, "You okay?"

Sasha offers a hand to help me up. "Did you hurt your arm again?" I feel fine, but it gives me a great idea. I grasp my right arm when I stand up. "Wow," I say. "That hurts."

Jarrett and Anthony stand back, mortified. The bell rings and they race into line. Mrs. Fedorchuk is on yard duty, and I see her lean over to speak to them.

"Maggie, did he really hurt your arm?" Sasha asks as we walk over to join the line.

"No," I say. "But Jarrett doesn't have to find out. If I hit him with both Project Romance and Plan Pain, he won't know what's happening."

Once we're in the classroom, morning announcements start. "The following people should come to the gym at recess," the principal says. He reads the first eight or ten names, and it's obvious he's calling out the people who are in the musical.

"Jarrett Johnson."

Anthony high-fives Jarrett.

"I don't care," I say to Sasha. "I'm probably not going to watch the musical anyway."

The principal reads out Alice's name and everyone cheers.

"I'm happy for her," I say. But I'm such a loser. It's bad enough not getting a lead role. What if I don't get a role at all? Will people laugh at me?

"Melissa Gardiner," the principal reads. "Maggie Ito."

Everyone cheers. "I told you!" Sasha says. "I'll sit in the front row every night."

"It's definitely not a singing role," I say. But I can't stop grinning. I got a part!

At recess, I go to the meeting in the gym. On the way in, I read the chart by the door where the roles are listed. I try to ignore Jarrett's name near the top beside Tin Man. Alice is Glinda the Good Witch, and further down I see my name beside Oz Lady. Except someone has crossed out "Maggie" and written "Magnolia" beside it.

I peer around the corner of the gym, and see Jarrett staring back at me, watching for a reaction. I give him none. But I pull the *girls suck* eraser out of my pocket and remove all evidence of Magnolia from the chart.

Alice walks up behind me and I point out her name. "Remember when we talked about who'd try out for the witch?" I ask.

"I didn't guess I'd be one of them," she says. "But I'll have fun being Glinda. She probably wears a beautiful gown."

"I was surprised you didn't get Dorothy. You take voice lessons, and you had a great tryout."

"At first I was disappointed. But I have two more years to audition for the lead. I thought about it over the weekend, and I'm happy just to be in the show."

"Me too," I say, and I'm surprised to realize that I mean it. I don't have a major role, but it'll be fun anyway. And I have a couple of lines that put me in the spotlight. "I can't believe I made it," I say. "I totally messed up the song. I must have done okay on the reading."

Alice laughs. "I signed up before you on purpose. I wasn't sure if you could sing, but I knew you'd nail the reading. You're a good actress and you're funny. I thought if I went first, I'd have a chance."

Out of the corner of my eye, I notice Jarrett staring at me. Might as well display those "good actress" skills. I frown and grasp my right arm as if it's aching. He twists around and looks in the other direction.

Back in the classroom, I tell Sasha about the meeting. She hugs me. "I'm proud of you!" she says. "You'll be the best Oz Lady ever."

Of course, I'm eating lunch at home because I'm grounded. But today I'm glad about it for two reasons. First reason: it's great to tell Dad about getting the role. We do our secret handshake, and then I call Mom at work to tell her.

And the second reason: it lets me prepare for the

afternoon session of Plan Pain.

When I return to school, Sasha, Alice, and Lauren examine the tensor bandage on my arm, and their eyes grow huge.

"I can't believe it! It's sprained again," Sasha says. "Jarrett's going to be in so much trouble."

"One of those things is true," I say.

"What do you mean?" Lauren asks.

"My arm's okay. I wanted to see what Jarrett would say if he thought he re-sprained my arm."

The girls laugh. "How do you come up with these ideas?" Alice asks.

The bell rings, marking the end of lunch. "I guess we'll find out what Jarrett thinks pretty soon," Sasha says. When we get to our lockers, Mrs. Fedorchuk is standing out in the hall. She sees my bandage immediately.

"Are you okay, Maggie?" she asks.

"I'm getting used to the pain."

Jarrett walks by on his way to class. He sees the bandage on my right arm. He jerks to a stop in the middle of the hall and his eyebrows shoot way up.

"Perhaps you can help Maggie this afternoon,"

Mrs. Fedorchuk says. "Can you carry her books for her? It's hard to do with a bandaged arm. You probably feel terrible, since it was you who knocked her down."

Jarrett doesn't say a word. He reaches for my books and follows me into the classroom. I could happily make this part of my daily routine.

The afternoon is fantastic. Jarrett carries my books to homeroom, to French, to my locker at the end of the day. Every time he does his duty with a glum expression and not a word. He does have a word or two for anyone who teases him, though:

Anthony: "Hey Jarrett, how's your girlfriend?"

Jarrett: "Shut up."

Lionel: "Can you carry my books too?"

Jarrett: "Get lost."

At the end of the day, he carries my books to my locker and dumps them at the bottom. As he walks away, I call out cheerfully, "Thanks, Jarrett! See you tomorrow!"

Today is the best day of my life.

I make my way back to the classroom. Mrs. Fedorchuk is there by herself, packing up some tests.

She turns to me. "Maggie, I'm sorry about your

arm. But by now, it must be used to healing. Maybe you won't need to wear the bandage after today."

Her eyes are twinkling and she shows her dimples. I smile back. Does she know everything?

"You wanted to ask my advice?" she continues.

I sigh. "Remember when I told you about the witch?"

Mrs. Fedorchuk nods.

"Everyone says I'm too old to believe in witches. But ever since I met her, everything started going wrong. And I haven't found something I'm best at. There's no other explanation — she must have put a curse on me."

One of the things I love about Mrs. Fedorchuk is that she doesn't laugh at me. "You feel like you've had some bad luck," she says. "But why would the witch want to curse you?"

Time to tell her the whole story. "When I was leaving, I accidentally knocked over a stand on the counter. After I left the shop, I realized I snagged an earring on my sweater. The curse is her way of getting revenge."

"If that's true, what do you think you should do?"

It's one of those questions that adults ask where you both know the answer. It's the answer I've been trying to avoid since I first visited the haunted house, the thing I'm most afraid of doing. "I guess I should take back the earring."

"Great idea."

I pick up my books, but I pause on the way out. "Do you think if I get rid of the curse, I'll find something that I'm best at?"

Mrs. Fedorchuk smiles. "Find something you love to do and do it. Don't worry if you're the best or the worst."

It sounds good, but I'm not sure. "If I do what I love, and do it as well as I can . . . what if I'm terrible at it?"

"Maybe you won't be great at first. But chances are, if you keep trying you'll get better. Sometimes it'll feel like a stretch. But that's how you can explore your limits and find out what you're truly capable of doing."

I keep going over that conversation throughout the week. Finding something I enjoy doing is the easy part. I love being in the musical — we had our first practice and I've already memorized my lines. It wasn't hard. Half of my lines are "Help!" or "Help! A lion!" Also, I get to hit the Cowardly Lion with an umbrella. I wish Jarrett was the Cowardly Lion.

And there are lots of other things I love to do. Like cooking. Now that I've mastered macaroni and cheese, there are a hundred recipes I can try. Maybe even croissants.

The hard part will be going back to the haunted house. But I have to do it. And this time, I'll actually talk to the witch.

Dear Maggie,

I'll be giving the creative writing projects back tomorrow, but I wanted to tell you how wonderful your story about the witch is. What an exciting confrontation! Your creativity really shines through.

Also, I enjoyed talking to you last Monday. Come in any time you'd like to chat.

Mrs. Fedorchuk

Dear Mrs. Fedorchuk,

It was fun talking to you, too. I've thought a lot about finding something I love to do, and not worrying about being best. It'll be hard, but I'm going to give it a shot.

Thanks for helping me realize that I need to take the earring back. It's the right thing to do.

Maggie

I had to wait two weeks until I wasn't grounded anymore, but finally the day has come. When I get home from school, Dad asks me to buy potatoes and carrots at the produce shop on Bloor Street. It's a perfect chance to visit Fresh Ink one last time.

I'm carrying one of Mom's worst cloth bags, the only one I can find. It's blue and it's covered in enormous white flowers. I'm pretty sure that she and Dad hid the decent ones, and that carrying this bag is part of my punishment.

I walk up the sidewalk to the haunted house again. The flowers have been torn from where they rotted in the planters, but in their place someone has shoved a few skeleton heads on spikes. All the way along the path are tombstones, with piles of earth and fallen leaves mounded around them. I know they're just Halloween decorations, but they give me a chill.

A skeleton hangs from the lamppost outside the door. The chains draped around its neck rattle as I brush by.

I've had this curse for two months, but it seems about a hundred years ago that I was last here. As I hesitate at the door, I realize I should have talked to the witch before I shopped. Then I could have scrunched up the bag and hidden it under my arm. Instead I have a hideous bag full of potatoes and carrots bumping up against my legs.

I open the door and walk in. Immediately I hear demonic laughter. I shriek, then notice that I've stepped on an electronic Halloween floor mat with sound effects.

Last time I was here, everything was new to me. I could hardly take in what I was seeing. The addition of a wrought-iron raven by the front desk and cobwebs hanging throughout the room make it even spookier. I shiver. Now it really does look like a haunted house. I can't believe I've come back.

I don't hear a warning cackle to let me know I'm in the presence of a witch. One minute I'm searching the tattoo images for a fenny snake, and the next I'm not alone. I whirl to face her.

There she is — The Witch of Bloor Street. Her hair's still deep red, and she still has a chunky lip ring. But this time she's wearing a pointy black hat and black robe, and is carrying a wand.

I gasp. "You really are a witch!"

"It's Halloween week," she says. "This is my go-to costume."

"Do you remember me?" I say. "I came in a couple of months ago and I knocked over the desk display."

"I do remember you. You ran out so quickly. I wondered what happened to you."

"Can we talk?" I say. "It's urgent."

She nods and checks the room to make sure no one else is around. "Let's grab a seat. I can chat as long as you want, unless another customer comes in."

We sit on the bench in the front room. The bag of vegetables is tucked away beside my feet. Now that I've come this far, I don't know what to say.

"I should introduce myself," the witch says, facing me. "I'm Violet, one of the tattoo artists."

"Violet?" I laugh. "Like the flower?"

"I guess you wouldn't expect me to have an old-fashioned name like Violet."

"That's not why I'm laughing. You see, my name is Maggie. Short for Magnolia."

We're facing the desk I bumped into last time. The display of earrings and nose rings is organized, exactly like it was before I knocked it over. An intricate dragon tattoo design hangs in front of the desk.

"I don't run into many other flower children," she says. "This practically makes us sisters."

I clear my throat. "If we're practically sisters, then I'll ask you a question." I feel my face blush, but there's no stopping. "Are you a witch?"

Violet bursts into the throaty cackle I remember from last time. "I'm a regular person. I just like looking different."

I shake my head. "I know it sounds crazy. But when I knocked over the stuff on the counter, I ran out because I was afraid. After I left, I realized one of the earrings had caught on my sleeve. My life has been so bad since then, I thought you put a curse on me." I pull the tiny broomstick out of my pocket and hand it to her.

She holds it in her palm and examines it. "A curse? Maggie, you have an incredible imagination!" She grins crookedly. "First, there's no curse. Good luck comes and goes, and so does bad luck. If you've had a string of bad luck, it means you're due for a turnaround pretty soon."

That sounds good to me. "And second?" I say.

Violet lifts the sleeve of her witch costume. On her wrist is a chunky silver bracelet with a broomstick dangling from it. It's a perfect match for the one I gave her. "When I didn't find its partner, I thought it was lost." She hands back my broomstick. "It's yours. Wear it any time you want a little magic in your life."

The door opens, and two teenage girls enter the room. They stop at the desk, and point at the dragon design, giggling.

"Sorry, I have to go," Violet says. We both stand, and I pick up my bag of vegetables. "Thanks for coming back," she says, smiling. As I leave, Violet approaches the girls and says in her best witch-like voice: "Can I help you?"

While I was inside, the wind blew the front pathway clean. This time as I leave, I'm careful to walk, not run, down the path. This time I don't trip and go sprawling on the sidewalk, losing a book in the middle of the road. This time I walk with dignity—well, as much dignity as possible when you're carrying a flowered bag full of vegetables.

As I walk home, I think about the things that Mrs. Fedorchuk, Alice, and Violet told me. Could it be that I have the best imagination?

I'm walking by the vegetable store when Jarrett emerges. He's carrying a beige cloth bag with the words "Recycling makes a difference" in huge red letters on it. It's even uglier than the bag I'm carrying.

He freezes when he sees me, and when he realizes I'm looking at his bag, he makes a face. "Mom asked me to get some vegetables."

I hold my bag up. "Must be a conspiracy."

We walk across Bloor Street together.

"Your arm's better," he says. "You're lucky you only had to wear the bandage for a day."

"It's a miracle," I agree.

We walk for about half a block, the silence broken by the occasional thump of a bagged potato knocking someone's leg.

Most of the lawns along this street are decorated for Halloween. The one we're passing has three gravestones in the yard, one with a skeleton's hand rising from the dirt in front of it. An orange-and-black witch on a broomstick is perched in the fir tree.

"I'm glad you're in the musical," he says.

I narrow my eyes, but it doesn't seem as if he's

setting me up. "You too," I say. "You'll be a great Tin Man."

"Thanks." He shifts his bag to the other hand. "You know, I heard the end of your audition. The part where you sang about me trying out for the musical."

My mouth goes dry. Jarrett has always teased me for no real reason. Now he has a reason to hate me. I might be safer living in that dragon sanctuary. "I'm sorry —I didn't mean —— I would never —"

He grins. "I like your lyrics better."

Maybe Jarrett isn't so bad. I might even admit that he's pretty funny. Or at least fenny.

We pause at the corner. "I'm turning here," Jarrett says. "See you tomorrow."

I turn onto my own street, glad to be close to home. If I help Dad peel the potatoes, he might let me bake chocolate chip cookies for dessert. I'll double-check the amount of butter I use. And after dinner, I'll call Sasha and tell her about Violet, and the broomstick, and my friendly encounter with Jarrett. Things are definitely looking up.

Dear Mrs. Fedorchuk,

I wanted to tell you before anyone else what happened after school today. I went back to the tattoo shop and found out that I wasn't cursed after all. The witch is actually a tattoo artist named Violet. She even let me keep the earring! See you tomorrow.

Maggie

P.S. I also found out that the Tin Man really does have a heart.

Acknowledgements

Maggie is inspired by books as much as I am! When I was writing this book, I took direct quotes from two other sources:

The Wizard of Oz: The Screenplay – Nigel Langley, Florence Ryerson and Edgar Allan Woolf
Delta Books, 1989

Macbeth – William Shakespeare
Penguin Books, 1994

In addition, Maggie refers to characters or situations from other books. These wonderful stories include:

Fablehaven – Brandon Mull
Aladdin Paperbacks, 2006

Harry Potter and the Philosopher's Stone – J.K. Rowling
Raincoast Books, 2000

The Hobbit – J.R.R. Tolkien
Harpercollins, 1998

What are your favourite books? Visit my website, www.bethpollock.ca, if you want to see more of my favourites or to let me know yours!

I gratefully acknowledge the Ontario Arts Council and James Lorimer & Company for their support through the Writers' Reserve program.